Plinky Witch and the Grand Halloween Scheme

Plinky Witch and the Grand Halloween Scheme

Liz Cooper

This is a work of fiction. Names, characters, businesses, places, events, locales, and incidents are either the products of the author's imagination or used in a fictitious manner. Any resemblance to actual persons, living or dead, or actual events is purely coincidental.

ISBN 978-1-956-783-001

Covers and Interior Art Credit:
Liz Cooper

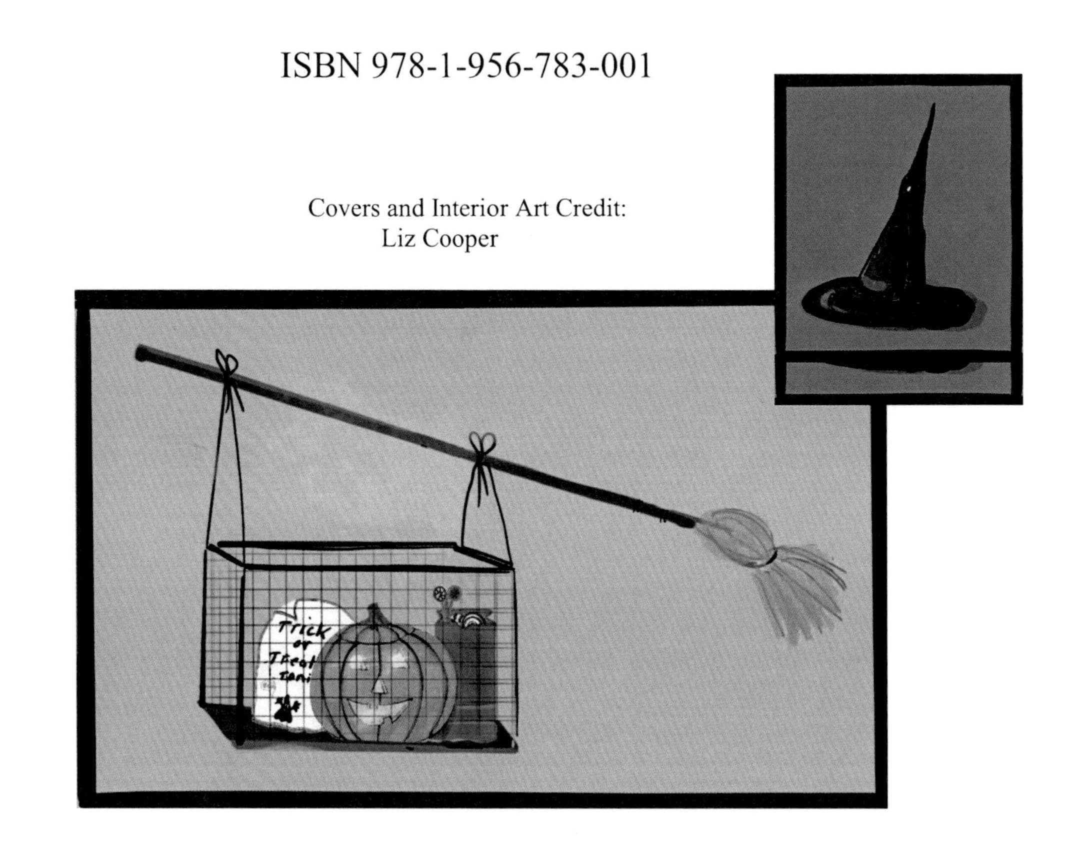

Plinky Witch had a thought one day,
while sitting on a stack of hay,
Halloween brings so much cheer—
it should come more than once a year!

I don't like waiting a whole year for Halloween to roll around, **Plinky thought.** *It would be much more fun if we could celebrate it every single day!* **She slid down the haystack and hopped onto her broomstick. She couldn't wait to share this exciting idea with her good friend, Glitch Witch.**

Glitch was impressed with Plinky's plan. "But if we want to start Halloween tonight, we'll need more help," Glitch said. "I'll call an emergency meeting of the Happy Broomsticks Club." She cast a telephone spell and called the other club members: Alora, Colette, Birdie, and Gracie.

The Happy Broomsticks

Glitch Witch

PRESIDENT

The Happy Broomsticks

Plinky Witch

MEMBER

The Happy Broomsticks

Alora Witch

MEMBER

The Happy Broomsticks

Colette Witch

MEMBER

The Happy Broomsticks

Birdie Witch

MEMBER

The Happy Broomsticks

Gracie Witch

MEMBER

In a flash, the club members appeared in Glitch's living room. After listening to the details, they voted on whether or not to carry out Plinky's scheme. There were six *yes* votes. It was unanimous! Halloween would start at nightfall that very night and take place every night—forever.

The group talked it over, made a list of items they would need, and decided what each of them would do.

Colette was the first to volunteer. “I’ll sew some fabulous costumes,” she said, waving her wand to make her favorite sewing basket appear. “You can’t go trick-or-treating without costumes."

Alora said, “We definitely need black cats. Some people say they bring bad luck, but they are actually quite lucky.”

Glitch used a special apple spell to make apples appear on the maple tree in her backyard. Juicy apples picked themselves and floated gracefully into her cauldron. Fresh hot apple cider would make a perfect Halloween snack.

Gracie visited the pumpkin patch. She was able to use a magical travel spell, which took no time at all. She returned instantly with a lovely pumpkin. It was just right for carving.

"This scary-hairy-rubber spider will do nicely for our trick," said Plinky. "I didn't even need any magic to make it!" She shook the stick and the rubber spider did a splendid little dance.

Birdie used her magic pens to create a list of all of the houses in town. "We don't want to miss out on any candy," she said.

Glitch was pleased with the club members' efforts. "Many hands make light work," she declared as she stirred her apple cider.

When the sun went down, the group was ready! The cats and birds even joined in the fun by dressing up. The clouds were gone, so it was going to be a beautiful starlit night. A full moon was predicted.

They stopped at the first house on the list and knocked. Mr. McMoore

looked rather surprised to see the Statue of Liberty, a bumblebee, an apple, a ghost, an astronaut, and a princess standing on his doorstep.

"Trick or treat," they yelled, and held out their goody bags.

Mr. McMoore said sadly, "I'm sorry, but I don't have any treats. I didn't realize that it's Halloween. I must have lost track of the days on my calendar." The group was disappointed but they didn't want to hurt his feelings. Plinky jiggled the dancing spider stick to cheer him up.

At the next house, they had the same problem. Mrs. Chen couldn't believe her eyes. "I thought Halloween was next month!"

Everyone was discouraged by the time they returned to Glitch's house. They had tried trick-or-treating at all the houses in town, and their goody bags were still empty.

After a good night's sleep, Plinky took charge. "This is no time to quit," she said confidently. "I have a new idea." She quickly shared her plan, and the six witches jumped into action.

They went to the town's best candy store, owned by Colonel S. Brandy, and bought everything he had.

They left the shop with a heavy wagon. It was filled with chocolates, licorice, lollipops, caramels, and every other kind of candy you could possibly imagine.

Plinky sat on the top of the pile to make sure they didn't drop anything. She sampled a rainbow lollipop just to make sure it was delicious. (It was.)

The pumpkin patch and the candle store were their next stops. Gracie spent the rest of the day carving lots of pumpkins while the others filled paper sacks with candy. The magic pens wrote a flyer to spread the word.

The broomsticks made special deliveries to the addresses on Birdie’s list.

After dark, the witches’ hard work paid off! A brightly lit Jack-O’-Lantern greeted them with a friendly smile on every porch in town.

Each time they yelled, “Trick or treat,” people dropped sweets into their goody bags until they overflowed. This success continued night after night. They collected so much candy that they ate it for breakfast, lunch, and dinner instead of regular food.

After a few weeks, everyone became tired of caramels, mints, chocolates, and other sweets.

Plinky finally said, “A carrot or squash would taste pretty good right now.” Glitch nodded in agreement, but there weren’t any vegetables in the house, only candy.

Other problems began to bother the group. Alora complained that her teeth were hurting. Even more shocking was the fact that their clothes no longer fit comfortably. Everyone had grown bigger—sideways, not taller.

Plinky Witch called another meeting of the Happy Broomsticks Club. "Maybe celebrating Halloween every night wasn't such a good idea after all," she announced. The others nodded in agreement.

"It's too much of a good thing," said Glitch.

Another vote was taken. It was unanimous. Halloween was over.

They immediately made an appointment with their favorite dentist to get their teeth checked.

That evening, Glitch and Plinky made a batch of vegetable soup. It was not only healthy but delicious as well. They poured the soup into six magical musical mugs. Each mug played a cheerful song every time one of the witches took a sip of soup.

The six witches were thrilled not to be eating any more candy. They were so relaxed that they didn't notice the queen, clown, ghost, and giant dog knocking at the porch door.

Nobody realized that the date on the wall calendar was *October 31st*.

October						
Su	M	T	W	Th	F	S
		1	2	3	4	5
6	7	8	9	10	11	12
13	14	15	16	17	18	19
20	21	22	23	24	25	26
27	28	29	30	31		

And that's the real Halloween!

About the Author

Liz Cooper enjoys writing funny stories about clever young people. Liz actually wrote and illustrated Plinky Witch and the Grand Halloween Scheme more than thirty years ago! She came across the manuscript while cleaning out a closet in 2020. She added dialogue to the story, which had been originally written in rhyme and re-drew the pictures.

Liz has had several interesting jobs because she loves to learn new things. She was an RN until she decided to become a schoolteacher. When she retired, she was serving as the school system reading supervisor. She is now a full-time writer.

Liz likes to kayak on the Potomac River. She also spends time making quilts and stained-glass projects. She lives in Maryland with her husband and two cats, Miss Max and Buffington. She has five grandchildren.

Visit:
www.LizCooperAuthor.Com
for more information about the
Plinky Witch Series
and Liz's other books